Who's In The Hall?
A Mystery In Four Chapters

by Betsy Hearne

ILLUSTRATED BY Christy Hale

GREENWILLOW BOOKS

An Imprint of HarperCollinsPublishers

To Joan Hall, whose hallways always
lead to an open door—B. H.

To my father,
Harold Charles Hale—C. H.

Black ink and watercolor paints were used to prepare the full-color art.
The text of this book is set in Myriad Tilt.

Who's in the Hall?
Text copyright © 2000 by Betsy Hearne
Illustrations copyright © 2000 by Christy Hale
All rights reserved.
Printed in Hong Kong by South China Printing Company (1988) Ltd.
www.harperchildrens.com

Library of Congress Cataloging-in-Publication Data
Hearne, Betsy Gould.
Who's in the hall? : a mystery in four chapters / by Betsy Hearne ;
illustrated by Christy Hale.
    p.   cm
"Greenwillow Books."
Summary: Three children, two babysitters, two dogs, a rat, and
a janitor finally get together and put an end to some confusion.
ISBN 0-688-16261-4 (trade).   ISBN 0-688-16262-2 (lib bdg.)
[1. Apartment houses—Fiction.   2. Babysitters—Fiction.]
I. Hale, Christy, ill.   II. Title.
[E]—dc21   99-042412   CIP
1 2 3 4 5 6 7 8 9 10   First Edition

ONE WAY

CAST OF CHARACTERS

Lizzy

Rowan

Wag

Ryan

Wave

Rat

Mother

Mother

Father

Grandmother

Nelly

Nick

Janitor

? ? ? ?
? ? ? ?
? ? ? ?

CONTENTS

RRRRRRRRRUFF!
RRRRRRRUFF!
IT!

CHAPTER 1

WAG AND WAVE

Lizzy had two dogs. One had a furry tail that wagged. The other had a feathery tail that waved. Wag was a happy dog who loved Lizzy most of all. Wave was a grouchy dog who loved Lizzy, and only Lizzy, and nobody else.

Lizzy and Wag and Wave lived in an apartment on the top floor of a tall building. They played tag on the roof. Sometimes Wag was IT and chased Lizzy and Wave. Sometimes Wave was IT and chased Lizzy and Wag. And sometimes Lizzy was IT and chased Wag and Wave around and around till they were all dizzy.

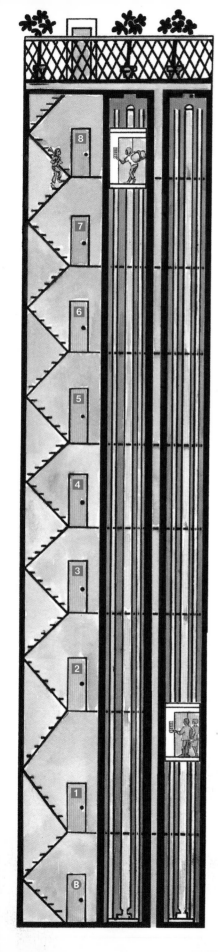

One day, Lizzy's father and mother kissed her good-bye and went off to work.

Lizzy's baby-sitter took all the sheets off the beds. Lizzy and Wag and Wave helped. Then the baby-sitter tied the sheets together into a big round ball.

"I'm going down to the basement, Lizzy. I'll be back as soon as I put these sheets into the washing machine."

"Can we come, too?"

"No. If I take you and the dogs, Wave will bark at everyone in the laundry room. Then the janitor will yell at me. If I take you and leave the dogs, Wag will bark at being left behind. Then also the janitor will yell at me. I'll be right back. Don't let anyone in. You can watch 'Mouse Patrol' on TV. Wag and Wave will take care of you." The baby-sitter closed the door and made sure it locked behind her.

Through the peephole Lizzy watched her go down the hall and get on the elevator with the big ball of sheets. Wag and Wave watched Lizzy watch the baby-sitter.

While the baby-sitter was going down in the elevator, someone else was coming up the stairs. Lizzy and Wag and Wave heard a knock at the door. Wag wagged her tail, but Wave barked a dark bark.

"Who is it?" called Lizzy.

"It's the janitor."

"the new janitor"

"Why not?"

"I'll come back later."

"It's the janitor," said a voice. Lizzy looked through the peephole into the hall. She saw a face.

"You're not the janitor," said Lizzy.

"I'm the new janitor," said the face. Lizzy could hear keys jangling. The face could hear Wave barking.

"Your baby-sitter said yesterday the sink was stopped up. I need to fix it."

"You can't come in," said Lizzy.

"Why not?" said the face.

"Because my dog will eat you up," said Lizzy.

"Oh," said the face. "Then I guess I'll come back later."

"Okay," said Lizzy. "My baby-sitter is busy now, anyway."

The face turned around and walked down the hall to the door under the big red EXIT sign. Lizzy and Wag and Wave could hear keys and footsteps echo down the stairs.

Wag kept wagging and Wave kept barking. Then Lizzy heard the elevator door open, footsteps in the hall, and a key in the lock. The door opened.

"Hi, honey," said the baby-sitter. "Is everything okay?"

"Everything is fine," said Lizzy. "Wag and Wave took care of me. Can we go up on the roof today and play tag?"

"Sure," said the baby-sitter. "Do you want to go now or wait till 'Mouse Patrol' is over?"

"We have to wait till the janitor comes back," said Lizzy.

"The janitor?" asked the baby-sitter.

"The one you told to fix the sink."

"I didn't tell anyone to fix the sink."

"The janitor told me you said to fix the sink."

"Someone was here while I went downstairs?"

"Yes, but I didn't let anyone in."

"Oh, Lizzy," said the baby-sitter. "You're a hero."

"Yes!" said Lizzy. "And Wave, too. She barked and barked! Wag just wagged her tail."

The baby-sitter hugged Lizzy tight, and Wag danced around them, wagging her tail.

"I am a hero and Wave is a hero and you are IT," Lizzy shouted at Wag, and she ran around and around the room with Wave at her heels and Wag chasing after them.

CHAPTER 2

ROWAN AND RYAN

Rowan and Ryan had a new room and also a new rat.
Rowan and Ryan had red hair, and the rat was black.

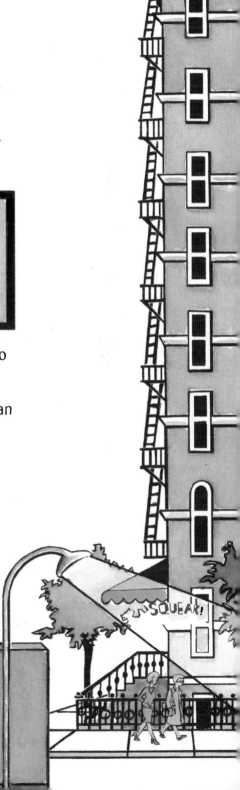

Rowan and Ryan had just moved from their old house into
the bottom floor of a tall building. The rat had just moved
from his old cage in the pet store to his new cage in Rowan
and Ryan's room on the bottom floor of the tall building.

On the first day they moved in, Rowan and Ryan's
mother and grandmother hired a new baby-sitter. They
stayed home to break him in, and show him the park,
and unpack boxes. On the second day, they kissed Rowan
and Ryan good-bye and went off to work.

"So what do you guys want to do today?" asked the new baby-sitter.

"I'm not a guy, I'm a girl," said Rowan. "I told you that yesterday. And I want to play with the rat."

"Yikes," said the baby-sitter.

"I want to watch TV," said Ryan.

"I'm with you, buddy," said the baby-sitter.

"I'm not your buddy," said Ryan. "I told you that yesterday. And I want to watch 'Rat Patrol.' I want to watch it all by myself."

"Yikes," said the baby-sitter.

Rowan went to play with the new rat in the new room. Ryan went to watch "Rat Patrol" on TV. The baby-sitter went to make himself a cup of Nerve Balm Herb Tea in the kitchen.

"Drat," said the baby-sitter. "The sink is still stopped up. I told the janitor about that when we came home from the park yesterday."

"Hey, Ryan," he called. "I'm going to see if I can find the janitor. This sink is still stopped up."

"I'm not Ryan, I'm Rowan."

"I thought Rowan was playing with the rat."

"We swapped. That rat is scared of girls."

"Maybe some girl bit him," said the baby-sitter.

"Very funny," said Rowan.

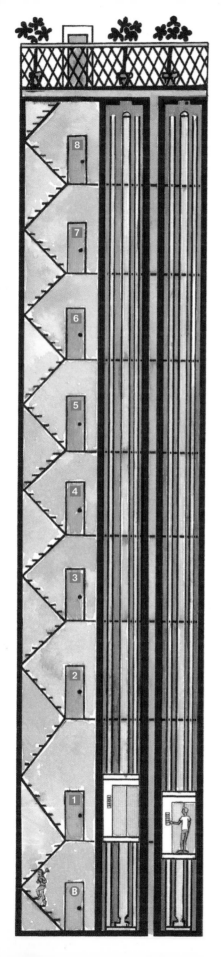

"Thanks for the compliment," said the baby-sitter. "I'll be right back. Don't let anyone in." The baby-sitter closed the door and made sure it locked behind him. Ryan played with the rat and Rowan watched "Rat Patrol."

While the baby-sitter was going down in the elevator to the basement, someone else was coming up the stairs from the basement. Rowan and Ryan heard a knock at the door.

"Who is it?" called Rowan.

"It's the janitor," said a voice. Rowan turned off "Rat Patrol" and looked though the peephole into the hall.

"Who is it?" yelled Ryan from the bedroom.

"The janitor," yelled Rowan.

Ryan came and looked through the peephole, too. Then Rowan looked again. They could see a face and hear keys jangling.

"I'm the janitor," said the face.

"How do we know that?" said Rowan.

"Your baby-sitter said yesterday the sink was stopped up. I need to fix it."

"You can't come in," said Ryan.

"Why not?" said the face.

"Because our rat will bite you," said Rowan.

"Oh," said the face.

"Then I guess I'll come back later."

"Okay," said Ryan.

"Our baby-sitter is busy now, anyway."

"Why not?"

"I need to fix it."

"Oh."

"I'll come back later."

The face turned around and walked down the hall to the door under the big red EXIT sign. Rowan and Ryan and the rat could hear keys and footsteps echo down the stairs. Then Rowan, Ryan, and the rat heard the elevator door open, footsteps in the hall, and a key in the lock. The door opened.

"Hi, guys," said the baby-sitter. "Is everything okay?"

"The janitor came," said Rowan and Ryan.

"Drat," said the baby-sitter. "I was in the basement looking for the janitor! But anyway, you did the right thing not letting anyone in."

"Yes, and we're bored," said Rowan and Ryan.

"Hey, I saw a kid running around with some dogs on the rooftop when I came here yesterday. Do you want to see if she'll play?"

"Sure, with the dogs!" shouted Rowan and Ryan, and they ran out the door to the elevator with the baby-sitter right behind them and the rat in Ryan's pocket.

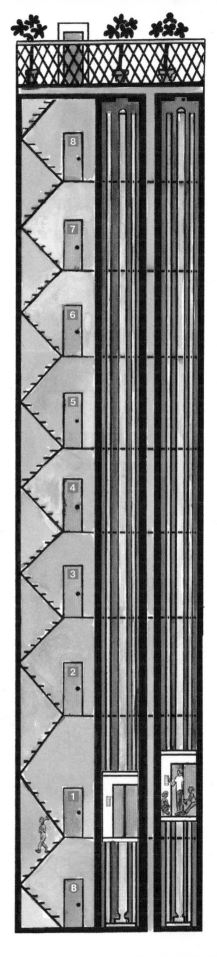

CHAPTER 3

NICK AND NELLY
AND WILLY-NILLY

"I'm bored," whined Lizzy.

"Don't whine, Lizzy," said the baby-sitter.

"I'm not whining," said Lizzy. "I just want to go up on the roof."

"Let's watch 'Mouse Patrol' first. Then we'll go up on the roof," said the baby-sitter. "It's going to be a long day."

"Stupid old 'Mouse Patrol,'" said Lizzy.

"No name-calling," said the baby-sitter.

"It's just a stupid old TV show," said Lizzy.

"You need somebody to play with," said the baby-sitter.

"I have Wag and Wave," said Lizzy.

"Somebody without a tail," said the baby-sitter.

Just then, there was a knock on the door. Wag wagged his tail, and Wave barked a dark bark.

"Maybe that's the janitor," said Lizzy.

The baby-sitter looked through the peephole into the hall.

"Who is it?" asked Lizzy.

"It has whiskers," said the baby-sitter.

"Let me look," said Lizzy.

Two beady black eyes looked back at her. A long nose twitched right into the peephole.

"That's not the same janitor," said Lizzy.

"No, I don't think so, either," said the baby-sitter.

"Hi, guys," said a voice. "We're from downstairs. I'm Nick the baby-sitter, and Rowan and Ryan wanted to know if you could play."

"With the dogs," said Rowan.

"Both dogs," said Ryan.

"Sure," said Lizzy's baby-sitter.

She opened the door and stuck out her hand.

"Hi, Nick. I'm Nelly, and this is Lizzy."

"And Wag and Wave," said Lizzy. Wag wagged his tail. Wave sat on his tail.

Lizzy stared at Rowan and Ryan.

"How do you tell them apart?" asked Lizzy.

"It's not easy," said Nick, "but the rat has whiskers." He shook Nelly's hand and said, "This is Rowan and Ryan. They just moved here."

"Welcome," said Nelly. "Come on in and close the door so Wag and Wave won't get out and bother the janitor."

22

"I wish I could find the janitor!" said Nick.

"He's always around here somewhere," said Nelly.

"He?" said Nick. He stared at Nelly. "I thought it was 'she.'"

"No wonder you can't find him," said Nelly. She stared back at Nick.

Rowan and Ryan and the rat stared at Lizzy.

"What's your rat's name?" asked Lizzy.

"Just Rat," said Rowan. "He's new."

"You have to name him," said Lizzy.

"No, we don't," said Ryan.

"Mouse Patrol" squeaked on the TV set.

"Let's watch 'Rat Patrol,'" said Rowan.

"It's not 'Rat Patrol,' stupid. It's 'Mouse Patrol,'" said Lizzy.

"No name-calling, Lizzy," said Nelly.

"Stupid yourself," said Rowan.

"No name-calling," said Nick.

"Your name is Stupid Yourself?" asked Lizzy.

"Lizzy!" said Nelly.

"Anyway, the show is called 'Mouse Patrol.' Everybody knows that," said Lizzy.

"We call it 'Rat Patrol,'" said Ryan. "We like rats better."

"Well, willy-nilly, they're all rodents," said Nelly.

"Willy-nilly?" asked Lizzy.

"Willy-nilly—like it or not," said Nelly.

"Yeah, willy-nilly, like it or not, they're all rodents. So why don't you guys name the rat?" said Nick. "Then it will feel special."

"Willy-Nilly," said Lizzy.

"Willy-nilly what?" asked Rowan.

"Not Willy-Nilly What. Just Willy-Nilly," said Lizzy. "Name the rat Willy-Nilly."

"Cool," said Ryan.

"Wag and Wave and Willy-Nilly," said Rowan.

"Wag and Wave and Willy-Nilly and Dizzy-Lizzy," said Lizzy.

"Wag and Wave and Willy-Nilly and Dizzy-Lizzy and Rowan and Ryan!" shouted Ryan.

"Wag and Wave and Willy-Nilly and Dizzy-Lizzy and Lowdown-Rowan and Ratty-Ryan and Nelly-Belly and Wicked-Nick!" shouted Nick.

"Can we go up to the roof and play?" shouted Lizzy.

"It might be a little crowded," said Nelly. "And shush up, or the janitor will yell at me."

Just then there was a knock at the door.

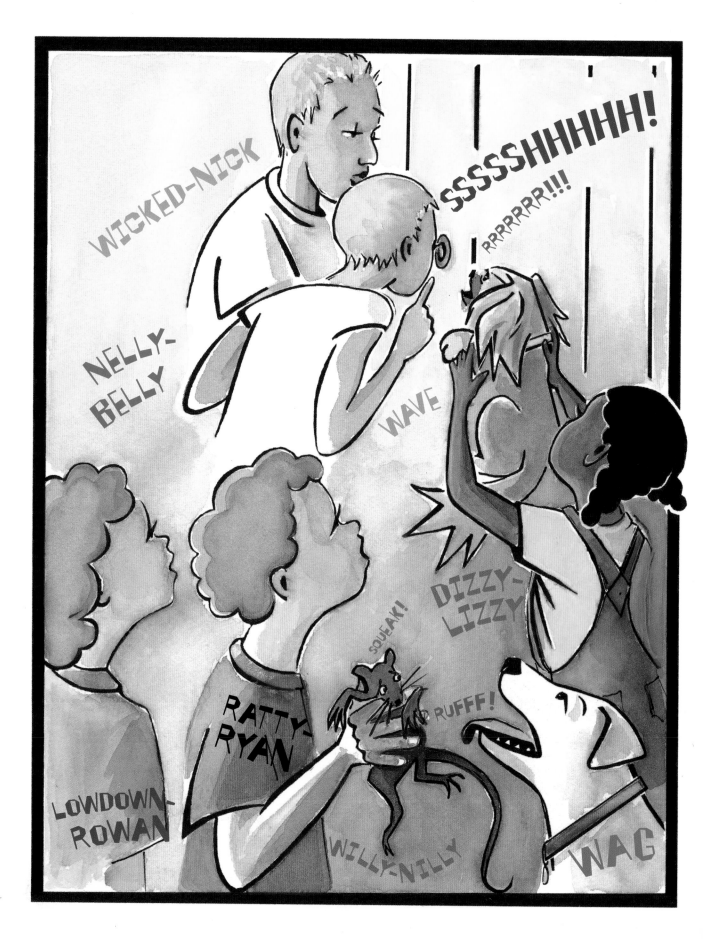

CHAPTER 4

?

"Uh-oh, we've been making too much noise," said Nelly.

"We have?" said Nick. "This is nothing. We could make a lot more noise if we tried."

"Yeah!" shouted Lizzy and Rowan and Ryan together.

"Shhhhhhhhh," said Nelly.

There was another knock at the door.

"Who is it?" shouted Lizzy and Rowan and Ryan and Nelly and Nick. Wag wagged his tail, and Wave barked a dark bark.

"It's the janitor," said a voice.

Nelly looked through the peephole into the hall.

"You're not the janitor," said Nelly.

"I'm the new janitor," said the face.

"I'M THE NEW JANITOR."

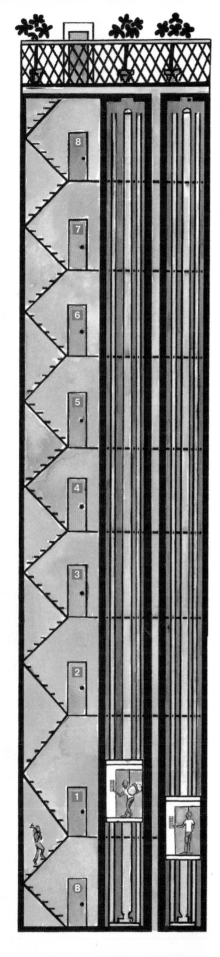

"Oh, now I see! You're right, he is a she," said Nelly to Nick. She opened the door. There stood the new janitor.

"Hi, I'm Nelly," said Nelly, "and this is Lizzy and Wag and Wave ..."

"And I'm Nick from downstairs," said Nick. "I talked to you yesterday. And this is Rowan and Ryan and Willy-Nilly."

"Oh, so it *was* you on the bottom floor!" said the janitor to Nick. "I thought at first it was her on the top floor. Sorry, there are a lot of people in this building. A lot of their sinks are stopped up, too."

"Not ours," said Lizzy.

"Nobody else has a rat," said Rowan.

"I hope not," said the janitor.

"How do you feel about dogs?" asked Nelly.

"As long as they're friendly," said the janitor. She held out her hand.

Wag wagged his tail and sniffed her fingers.

"Nice dog," said the janitor.

Wave sat on his tail and did not move.

"Oh, well," said the janitor, "you can't win them all."

"I tell you what," said Nick. "If you do the sink, we'll do the park."

"It's a deal," said the janitor. "And by the way, my name is Jo."

"Yo, Jo!" shouted Lizzy.

"Not so loud, Lizzy!" said Nelly.

"That's okay. I like kids," said Jo, "so long as they're friendly."

"So, Jo, I'm Rowan," said Rowan.

Jo smiled.

"So, yo, Jo, do you sew?" asked Ryan.

"Do you mow the lawn low?" asked Rowan.

"And row your boat in the stinky sinks?" asked Lizzy.

"WHOA!" said Nick.

"Let's GO," said Nelly, and she towed them all out the door. Wag wagged, Wave waved—then Wag and Wave and Dizzy-Lizzy and Lowdown-Rowan and Ratty-Ryan and Nelly-Belly and Wicked-Nick skitter-scattered to the park while Willy-Nilly watched Jo fix the stinky sink.

THE END